THE ADVENTURES
OF MONTY HORTON (#1)

A Space Adventure

To Winnie
God bless!
Auntie
Mary

BY MARY ASHUN © 2008

Introducing the Monty Horton Series:

Students (and teachers!) the world over often have trouble explaining major scientific concepts that have shaped our understanding of the universe. Scientific greats such as Einstein, Archimedes, Marie Curie, Newton, Leonardo Da Vinci and others are somewhat known by students at the High School level but with scientific literacy among younger children at a dangerously low point, the Monty Horton Series will use fiction, to awaken the desire to know more, learn more and understand more. Each 'episode' will take a particular scientist and a concept for which that scientist is known and weave a fictional adventure around that concept, thereby increasing scientific literacy by creating real-world connections. This series is appropriate for the 8 – 12 year group and can be used as a library book, a read-aloud adventure for the younger grades or a literacy builder during the course of the school year. Its use of language as a means of conveying scientific concepts broadens its appeal and the myriad of memorable characters within its pages ensures that all children will identify with one or more of the characters in the book.

In this episode, Monty experiences Einstein's theory of Special relativity...in Space!

M. Ashun

The Adventures of Monty Horton

A Space Adventure

ISBN 1440437068

EAN-13 9781440437069.

Edited by Angela P. Bick

Cover Art by RACUD
www.globalillustration.com

Dedicated to Abeyku, Kwamena, Jojo and all the frustrating yet adorable boys I have had the honour of teaching. May you grow up to be wonderful young men…and discover new worlds!

CHAPTER ONE

The Grade Six Science Fair was set for next week Friday. The thought of explaining his project for the gazillionth time to the gazillionth person who walked by filled Monty Horton with dread. He wondered what would happen if he forgot the 'main idea' of his topic. He was sure his teacher, Miss Jenkins, would go nuts and maybe send him to the office and then. . . Miss Walpole, the Vice Principal with weird poofy hair, would push her glasses down her nose and peer at him like he was an insect.

"Now. What *have* we been up to, Mr. Horton?"

Mmm...nothing? Monty would think.

Monty's thoughts were put on hold when his best friend Mason caught up with him. Mason was cool. So cool there was no other word to describe him. He had Game ProUltimate (of course!) and he would definitely be getting the upgrade when it came out. Mason had an older brother called Jason and he was in a band. Whenever Monty came over, he got to listen to absolutely awesome music and even practice on Jason's guitar, which made Monty think he'd like to be a guitarist for a band someday.

"Hey, you done your poster?" asked Mason.

"Yah right," Monty drawled. "When was the last time I did anything on time, huh?"

They laughed and walked into Room 208, the wacky room where the boys suspected Miss Jenkins stayed overnight. It was a room that made you wonder if you might make a mind-boggling discovery and become the world's youngest Nobel Prize winner! Miss Jenkins loved talking about famous scientific discoveries. Most of the time though, the last thing Monty wanted to know was why Antonie Van Leeuwenhoek called the little things he saw under his microscope 'animalcules'!

"Now class," Miss Jenkins began, "we are going to put the finishing touches to our Science Fair projects today. I dare say—for some of you—" and with this, she looked at Monty, "it will be the *beginning* touches, yes?"

Sniggers could be heard around the room as eager beavers like Mary and Kendall looked lovingly at their Science Fair posters, all done and ready to be shipped off to their own Nobel Prize committee. Marlon and Cody were staring into space; it was obvious they still hadn't come up with a topic, let alone a main idea. At least Monty had a topic and an approach. They just hadn't made it to a poster board!

"We will have a quick run-through of everyone's topics and main ideas and then you will have some class time to work. I will come around and see what you've done."

That wasn't good, Monty thought. *What on earth was he going to tell Miss Jenkins?* Before he had time to think, Miss Jenkins fixed him with a steely look.

"Mr. Horton, what is your title and main idea?"

"Umhh…" he stuttered. "My title is 'Special Relativity.'"

"I see. 'Special Relativity,' huh?" Miss Jenkins said. "And what is the main idea here? What are you going to be studying? Why do you want to study that? Is there any special significance to that topic?"

Whoa, chill, Monty wanted to say. *You're way way ahead of me!. . .*

"Ummhhh…I dunno."

"That's not good enough, young man. You have had since September to think of all of this and ask for help. You and I need to have a talk after school."

No! Monty thought. *That won't work. I'm supposed to be playing softball with Mason and the other guys!*

He scrunched his face up and put his head on the desk in despair as he listened to the other topics his classmates were studying.

"My topic is 'Aneurysms,'" Kendall was saying, "and my main idea is to look at how people get them and how we can prevent them."

"Very good," said Miss Jenkins. "Abdul?"

"My topic is 'Organic Foods.' I will be looking at how much they cost, why people think they are better and whether we should really bother with them."

"I can't wait to see what you have uncovered already, Abdul! Marlon?"

There was only the briefest of pauses. "Why is a football shaped the way it is? If it was another shape, would it zip through the air when the quarterback throws it? What has shape got to do with aerodynamics? That's what I'm wondering," Marlon added, sounding a bit breathless.

Miss Jenkins and all the students were shell shocked! Marlon saying anything that made sense was unheard of. It was so surprising that Monty raised his head, just to make sure he had heard right. Everyone was staring with astonishment at Marlon, who—it seemed—had one more thing to add.

"So, my topic is going to be 'Shape and Air Resistance in the NFL.'"

This was bad, Monty thought. *Even Marlon the Melon had a topic. . . a really good topic, and now*

Monty was the one feeling like a melon. . .a bigger and emptier one than Marlon used to be!

"Before you leave, class," Miss Jenkins said, "don't forget to give me your permission slips for our field trip tomorrow if you haven't already done so. Without the signed form from your parents, you won't be permitted to attend."

The rest of the day passed in a blur. After his meeting with Miss Jenkins, Monty was feeling miserable. She told him that if he didn't do an excellent job on his Science Fair project, his chances for passing Grade Six were slim. He felt so depressed all he wanted to do was go home and talk to his dad on the webcam and listen to his stories about work at the mines in Chile. He wished his dad didn't have to travel so much. And, though he'd never admit it to Miss Jenkins, Monty wondered if it was easier to become super lazy when his dad wasn't around to encourage and tease him.

He wished his dad would come home.

CHAPTER TWO

Monty tossed and turned that night. How on earth was he going to come up with an amazing Science Fair project? He wanted it to be better than Marlon's! And, more than anything, he wanted Miss Jenkins to be proud of him again. . . the way his Grade One teacher had been when he showed up the first week of school reading at a Grade Three level!

Should I change my topic? He knew the library was full of books on space, but what did relativity have to do with space? Monty found it so intriguing. *Why did Miss Jenkins talk about Albert Einstein and relativity in one sentence?* He juggled these questions in his mind till he drifted off to sleep and had a very, very strange dream.

The field trip to the Canadian Space Agency was over, and all the Grade Six students from Kingsway Middle School were packing up their stuff and getting ready to go home. Room twenty-three was no different as Monty, Mason and Earl threw all their clothes back into their overnight cases.

"Hey, did you take my backpack?" Monty asked Earl.

"Of course not! Why would I?"

"I dunno, maybe you like my snacks?"

"Well, I haven't got it!" Earl replied, indignantly.

After some more fussing, they found everything except Monty's backpack. It had likely been left in the shuttle during the tour, he thought. He'd probably have just about enough time to run over, pick it up and get back on the bus. He whispered something to Mason, while Earl looked at the two of them suspiciously.

"Whaaat?" Monty asked, innocently.

Earl Parton looked as though he thought they were making plans to blow up the cabin, but he didn't say anything.

In the parking lot, Miss Jenkins read through the attendance list. As soon as she had passed his name, Monty squeezed past her and only pretended to get onto the school bus. Luckily for him, his teacher did not notice him sneaking back into the crowd and making his way towards the huge buildings that they had toured earlier. He had a plan.

Miss Jenkins had a warm smile and wild hair, which made her every child's favorite teacher. She ran down the list again, looked through the bus, and thought she saw everyone there. They had been instructed to wait for ten minutes in the bus and then drive slowly to a site near an abandoned area around Mirabel Airport, where the space shuttle would be launched. Miss Jenkins let the class talk and holler while they waited.

Mason, however, couldn't stop fidgeting. *Where was Monty?* He was supposed to be back by now. The plan was to tell Miss Jenkins after ten minutes. Before Mason had time to get really worried, Cody challenged him to a game on his PSP and Mason completely forgot about Monty. He became so engrossed in the game that he didn't feel the bus moving. It backed slowly out of the agency complex and along a series of side roads that led to a safe distance from the launch site.

Mason lost the first game to Cody and groaned in exasperation. Then he sat bolt upright. *Oh no!* he thought. *Monty's not on the bus and we've left. What am I gonna do? Do I tell now?* Mason didn't like being responsible for anything – only grown-ups had to be responsible! The bus finally came to a stop outside a sheltered area and Miss Jenkins pointed to the enormous shuttle. All the kids pressed their faces against the glass windows.

"Wow—"

"Cool—" many students murmured.

"Yes, I know. Isn't it fascinating?" Miss Jenkins said brightly. "The launch will take place in about fifteen minutes, so everyone sit tight, okay?"

By this time, Mason thought he was going to explode with fear. He gathered enough courage - barely - to walk slowly to the front of the bus.

"Miss Jenkins?" he whispered.

"Yes, Mason," Miss Jenkins said abruptly, turning around.

"Well, there's a sort of problem. . . ." he trailed off miserably.

Oh no, he thought. *Here goes.* He blurted out the next sentence like he was staring down a pack of wolves hungry for his blood.

"Monty's not here!"

"What?" Miss Jenkins shrieked, startled.

"Monty's not here!" Mason repeated.

"I heard you the first time. What do you mean, he's not here?"

The whole story came out. Miss Jenkins looked like she might faint. Mrs. Otto and Mr. Parton, the parent volunteers, looked like lightening had struck them—their faces were white and bloodless.

"Oh!" Miss Jenkins exclaimed, "this boy will be the death of me!"

She took out her cell phone and dialed the Education Desk at the Centre. By this time, all the kids on the bus knew what was going on and the annoying ones were singing "Monty's in trouble, Monty's in trouble, na na na na naa."

As Miss Jenkins spoke to the Education Officer, it was difficult to tell from her face what was going to happen. She looked angry, of course, but also frightened and a little exhausted. She turned off the cell phone and the whole bus fell quiet.

"We can't leave the launch site now," she said, in a softer voice, "because everything has to be still during a launch. They are, however, going to page him all over the building. They'll find him."

Mason walked back to his seat and wished he had said something sooner. *Where on earth was Monty?*

CHAPTER THREE

Monty, meanwhile, was in one of the compartments that looked like a cabin in the living quarters of the shuttle. He went in and out of a few rooms, trying to remember where he had left his backpack. He got frightened when he looked at his watch and realized that fifteen minutes had gone by already, and he still hadn't found the bag.

Tired and angry with himself for being so silly, he looked straight ahead and saw a shiny silver door with the sign "AUTHORIZED PERSONNEL ONLY ALLOWED HERE." *Authorized? What was that?* He decided to go in. After all, he wasn't planning on being too long. He opened the door slowly and realized that it was very heavy. He quickly looked around and saw no one, so he went inside. *Maybe someone saw my backpack and put it here so they would remember to take it back to the front desk.*

As soon as Monty entered the room, the door slammed shut behind him with a huge thud. *Whoa!* he thought, *that's not cool.* He started snooping around, looking high and low for a backpack that looked like his. He couldn't find it, so he headed back towards the door. For a moment, he thought he wasn't seeing straight. He'd never seen a door that didn't have a knob on the inside. That meant it could only open from the outside. . . .

Yiiikkkkkeeeessssss!!

Okay, calm down, he told himself sternly. *Take a deep breath.* Monty looked at the door again and ran his hands all over it, as far up as he could. *Now this is bad,* Monty thought. All of a sudden, he felt the ground beneath him start to move. *Is this an earthquake? Well, maybe an earthquake will tear the door down and let me out of here—*

Before he knew what was happening, Monty was thrown to the far side of the room.

He barely managed to open his eyes before a box fell on top of him. Then he got up slowly and looked around. Just after he realized that he was in some sort of compartment, he felt the floor moving again. This time, however, the movement wasn't violent; it was chugging along, sort of like a train.

Okay, Monty thought, *it's moving somewhere and now I've really got to get out of here!* He moved to the door again and started pounding very hard on it.

"Let me out of here!" he screamed at the top of his lungs.

"Somebody let me out of here!"

"Can anyone hear me?"

"I need help!"

No one came, but the room or house or whatever it was kept on moving. For the next thirty minutes, according to his watch, it did not stop.

This was bad. Where on earth was he and where was he going? As he sat on the floor of the room, afraid he'd fall again if he stood up, he wondered how he had gotten himself locked up in this creepy place with no food, no water, no friends, no hand-held gaming system and no way out!

"Even Marlon wouldn't have done something this stupid!" Monty said ruefully.

Monty's next thought was that he must be dreaming. *Of course! No way this is real.* He tried to slow his heartbeat down and so he could think. That was incredibly hard!. The movement had stopped, so maybe someone would come rescue him. *What should I do?* He decided that the wisest thing was to sit and wait. Meanwhile, he was really getting hungry.

He decided to search the boxes, so he took them down one at a time. The first one had a whole lot of papers and they all had to do with space. *Duh!* Not surprising, as this was a Space Centre. The next box had some packets of pink and cream coloured cubes. *Mmmm*, he thought, *I wonder what they are?* Being more curious than Curious George, Monty opened one packet (it *did* say edible on the outside) and put the contents in his mouth.

"Whoa!" he said.

This thing tasted awesome. It melted in his mouth, just like. . .ice cream! This was cool. He decided to eat a little bit more and then continue snooping around. Just as he started on the second packet, he heard a 'hey-everyone-listen-to-me' kind of voice through an invisible speaker.

"All crew are expected to be in their positions for take-off in ten," the voice said.

"Ten what?" Monty wondered. He was getting annoyed. First, he got a box dropped on his head, and now someone was talking about take-off. Take-off in ten, whatever that meant.

"Oh well," he said, "maybe after take-off, someone will come and look for me or at least for some stuff in this room, and then I can get out and go home with the class."

He continued pigging out on the food in the packets, and then the authoritative voice spoke again.

"All systems ready for takeoff in ten, nine, eight, seven, six, five, four, three, two, one, blast off! God speed, crew of the *Experience*."

To say the earth moved is an understatement! Monty had the most magnificent, brain-numbing and brain-blowing experience of his life! His head was spinning, his throat felt like it was on top of his head and his legs seemed to be on the other side of the room – he couldn't feel them at all. To top it off, he was thrown from where he was sitting on the floor, against one wall and then back to where he was sitting. His eyes felt like they were popping out of his head and his stomach wanted to explode. In fact, it did and all the food he had ever eaten in his life (at least, the food that wasn't absorbed into his body yet) came flying out – at about five hundred kilometres per second! That was faster than the bullet train in Japan!

He sat in all the gloop thinking that the worst had passed—when it happened again and again, until Monty started wishing he were dead! For a minute, he thought he might actually be dead, but then he realized he couldn't be because he couldn't see Grandma Gertrude and Grandpa Peter. They would be around in the next life; he was sure of it.

After lying down in shock and surrounded by lots of barf for about an hour, Monty slowly wiped his face with a clean part of his shirt and tried hard to think with what was left of his brain. He must have been on something that was traveling fast. What could that be? Think, think, think. *Okay, so I'm at the Space Centre and we came here to watch the shuttle launch and—*

"Yikes," he said weakly. "I'm on the crazy shuttle."

This…wasn't part of the plan!

CHAPTER FOUR

He couldn't believe it even after he said it. He pinched himself to make sure he wasn't sleeping and then groaned loudly. This was turning out to be one wacky field trip. His mom would definitely wring his neck, for sure—if it was still on his head after this. He wouldn't be home when she got back from work and then—oh dear. She'd hear that he was trapped on a shuttle way above the earth—in space! He couldn't think of anything worse. *Although, what if I'm stuck in orbit for the rest of my life? That would take the prize!*

Since he'd retched every single thing he'd eaten in his life (at least it felt like it), Monty was starving and feeling very weak. *I'm certainly not going to eat any more of that pink stuff, but what else is there?* As he wondered what to do next, he stretched out on the cold hard floor and prayed he'd wake up from this nightmare…

After what seemed like ten hours, he heard some footsteps. With what little energy he had left, he crawled to the door. He waited for it to open, but the footsteps faded along with the voices.

"Oh no," he groaned loudly. This was worse than being stranded on a deserted island. There was a loud sound that kept making his ears feel funny—like he was in a thousand airplanes at once or something. Monty started to pray.

"Dear God, if you're there, please listen to me, okay? I'm really in deep trouble here, and I'm hungry too. I wish there was some food to eat. Can you make some? Yeah, okay, cool. I'm waiting, God. Amen."

No food appeared. Well, maybe God was finishing HIS dinner or something. *Whatever.* Maybe he was with some friends. As he sat there wondering what God could be doing when he was in so much trouble, Monty set his chin and decided to use his last bit of energy to push the door down. He pushed and shoved and heaved. Pretty hard work it was. After ten minutes, he needed a break.

That's when he heard the voices again. This time, they got much louder, and then he felt the heavy door start to move.

He jumped up so quickly that he slipped on his untied shoelaces, still smothered with gunk from his stomach. He moved towards the door and waited with his arms outstretched. He was so excited that he was ready to hug anything that walked in through the door. *Although, I hope it's not Mrs. Brandenburg, the school secretary!*

The door opened and there were three big men standing in front of him. They looked at him and he looked at them. Monty couldn't help himself: he screamed!

"Hey, calm down. Who are you and what are you doing here?" one of the men asked, not unkindly. He had dark, greasy hair.

Monty screamed again.

The men looked at each other and the one with the bald head came towards him, then bent over, and picked Monty up! He felt like he was a hundred feet in the air, this guy was so big!

They carried him down a hallway and through huge double doors that closed so silently Monty wasn't even sure they had passed through any doors. The man put him on a bed that was stuck to the wall and they all towered over him, daring him to speak.

"Ummm, hhh, ummm, my name is Monty . . . you know . . . M-O-N-T-Y," he stammered slowly.

"Hi, Monty," said the one who had carried him. "My name is Captain Edmonds and this is Officer Kirkpatrick," pointing to the greasy-haired guy.

Captain Edmonds turned to the third man and said, "This is Officer Ogden. Now, we're done with our introductions, how about you give us yours?"

"Oh boy, it's a really long story," Monty said, stalling.

"That's okay," Officer Kirkpatrick said, "As you can tell, we're far away from earth. We've got all the time in the world."

The astronauts continued staring at him. Monty didn't think he'd like the Ogden guy. He looked like the kind of scary dude who bullies kids and takes away their candy. Officer Kirkpatrick and Captain Edmonds looked friendlier, so he decided to tell his story to them, and pretend Ogden wasn't there.

Heart beating wildly, Monty explained as best as he could how he'd ended up on a shuttle to outer space.

"I woke up this morning feeling good, jumped out of bed, checked the clock and went back to sleep again. I thought I could snatch about three minutes and 24 seconds more before Mom started screaming for me to get dressed for school.

"That's when I remembered—we were leaving for the school trip today! For a few moments I wasn't sure whether I'd given the permission slip to my mom to sign or not. If I hadn't, it would be a disaster. I jumped out of bed for the second time that morning and rushed to my back pack. Inside, buried quite deep, beside the half-eaten peanut butter and jelly sandwich was THE TRIP LETTER! I was going to be in so much trouble...I just knew it. Who else on this planet could be so stupid? *Okay—think!* I ordered myself. Do I tell Mom now, do I call dad in Chile or do I call both of them when I get to Montreal and say that I'm not coming home?

"I'm sure you realize that this was a very tough decision. If I told her now, it was certain that I wouldn't be allowed to go. On the other hand, would she sign the slip without noticing what it was for? It was time for some deep concentration, and I knew just where to go to find that. Into the washroom I went, and when I was done, I walked down the stairs with determination.

'Mom, can you sign this for me, please? It's for school.'

"Luckily, my mom was in such a rush to get to work and to pack my lunch bag that she took the sheet and signed it without looking. I held my breath until she was finished.

'Thanks, Mom. You're the best!' I said with relief.

'Make sure you take your lunch and don't forget to lock the door before you get onto the school bus. See ya after school at 4:30 okay?'

'Yeah, sure Mom.'

"I watched her go out the door and then I sped towards my bedroom like lightening. *Quick, time to pack some warm clothes. Where was the list of things to bring?* I looked in that incredible backpack again and found the orange coloured sheet titled Student Trip Essentials: Canadian Space Agency.

"By eight o'clock, I had packed a huge bag full of clothes, my brand new hand-held gaming system and some Archie comics. Then I sat down at the table to write my *Last Will and Testament.* Mason told me that his parents were writing their Wills—in case something happened to them, they wanted to make sure that the right people got the right stuff. Although, I was taking along all the things I loved dearly. Still, it couldn't hurt to write one. After ten minutes, this is what I had:

"LAST WILL & TESTAMENT OF MONTY HORTON (11 YEARS OLD)
I would like to say that I don't have much to give away but what I do have, I give to my mom and Mason. Mason can have all the fun stuff like my games (though with his upcoming Game ProUltimate upgrade, he might just take mine to the Salvation Army Donation Drop box) and Mum can have all my old clothes and everything else in my room. Also, I love you Mom and Dad and I never meant to be this silly – I just forgot that we were going to be away on a school trip today, but I'll be back in three days okay?
Signed, Monty Horton."

The officers chuckled, grinning at Monty. He continued his story.

"I went downstairs, dragging my huge bag, and placed the Will by the door so that Mom would see it. At that moment, I heard the school bus drive up and I had to rush out the door, almost forgetting to lock it

behind me. I remembered just in time and ran back to
lock it. The bus driver, Mr. Jepson, started honking.

'Ok, ok,' I muttered.

"I got into the bus and found a seat as far away
from Mr. Jepson as possible and started thinking
about how much fun I was going to have on this trip."

CHAPTER FIVE

"Miss Jenkins was reading down the class list as we stood outside near the big blue bus that was going to take us all the way to Montreal.

'Mary Asare?'

'Here.'

'Abdul Khalid?'

'Here.'

'Abdul, do you have your permission slip here? I didn't get it earlier, did I?' Miss Jenkins asked.

'Yes, you did, I gave it to you yesterday before recess.'

'Monty Horton,' said Miss Jenkins next, raising her head to look around the group.

'Here,' I said.

'And your permission slip, Mr. Horton?' Miss Jenkins said tersely.

'Hey,' I whispered to Mason, 'watch this.'

"I looked in my shirt pocket, checked the cargo pockets on my pants, put my backpack down and started removing every single thing out of my bag—individually.

'Mr. Horton, we're not going to sit around here while we wait for you to look for a slip that should have been in two weeks ago. I suggest that you go over to the office and—'

'Got it!' I shouted loudly, pulling the permission slip out of the back pocket of my pants.

"Miss Jenkins grabbed the slip and made a point of inspecting the signature like she thought it was fake. Satisfied that it was genuine, she added it to the pile of permission slips by her side and continued down the list.

'She's so mad at you, eh?' Mason noted.

'Yeah, I know,' I said, smiling.

"I didn't tell Mason that I know Miss Jenkins likes me and all she wants is for me to be a little bit more mature. At least that's what she says ALL THE TIME.

"When the attendance list was complete, we made our way to the bus, pushing each other aside and sticking twigs in the girls' hair. We managed to get into the bus with all our legs and arms intact and Miss Jenkins took another run down the list. When she was satisfied that everyone was on board, she turned to the bus driver and the other two parent supervisors and spoke in a lighter tone.

'Let's start the torture – on to Montreal!'

"Barely had we pulled out of the schoolyard when we heard a whimper from the middle part of the bus. Miss Jenkins turned abruptly to see Jennifer Meadows looking like a frightened little mouse. Miss Jenkins walked to her side, bent down and whispered to her.

'What's wrong Jennifer? Missing home already?'

'No, Miss Jenkins, I just forgot to use the washroom.'

"Miss Jenkins looked frustrated and walked over to the front of the bus. She whispered to the bus driver, who nodded, and then she walked back to Jennifer's seat.

'The bus driver is going to stop at the nearest fast food restaurant, and you can go inside, okay?'

"After about ten minutes, the bus driver saw a Burger King and pulled into the parking lot.

'Wow, cool! Miss Jenkins, is everyone getting a whopper?' shouted Marlon Kennedy, a kid with a head like a watermelon. His nickname was Marlon the Melon…naturally.

'Of course not. Now listen, class. We're stopping here to give everyone a chance to use the washrooms here IF they haven't used the ones at school. You've got to make it quick and don't even think of buying anything. You're not supposed to have that much money on you—'

'That's what she thinks,' Mason whispered to me.

'—and there'll be many nice souvenirs at the Space Agency.'

"Before Miss Jenkins could finish her sentence, an avalanche of smelly sneakers, greasy hair and bubble gum bubbles descended on her. She got out of the way as quickly as possible, looking astonished. Everyone was out of the bus!

"She followed us into the restaurant. Mason and I headed straight to the boys' washroom. Miss Jenkins waited faithfully in the lobby with Earl's dad, Mr. Parton, who was one of the parent volunteers. After 15 minutes, when we still hadn't come out, Mr. Parton came in to get us. I tried to sneak into the Burger King line-up after that, but he stopped us. Soon enough, we were on the way to Montreal again. It looked like Miss Jenkins was wondering if she should have her head checked for planning this trip!

"Along the winding highway 401 we went, and while some kids marveled at the stretches of land they saw, others couldn't stop talking about *The*

Simpsons, the latest fashions, or the latest games just released by Sony and the Game Pro. Miss Jenkins looked sleepy and tried to put her head back, but not before checking who was behind her. She probably didn't want to end up with bubble gum in her hair!

"We soon passed Kingston, and Miss Jenkins casually mentioned that this was where she had gone to school—at Queen's University.

'Wow,' Megan Patricks said, 'is that a university?' "Megan was like a cheeseburger with no cheese—not too quick in the thinking department".

'Duh,' said Kerrie Macy, another cheeseburger. 'Of course it's a university; it's a big building, Megan.'

"I saw Miss Jenkins cover her eyes; she was probably dreaming of being on a deserted island, surrounded by biographies about her favourite famous scientists. It was just last week, when were learning about Einstein, that she mentioned something about his theory of time contraction. I didn't really understand it, but it sounded very cool".

"She took a folder out of her purse and a yellow insert fell out. She read it quickly, and started to smile widely. Then she stood up".

'I am pleased to announce that our class will— besides the usual tours and experiments at the

Agency—be allowed to witness the first Canadian Shuttle launched into Space.'

'Wow!'

'Cool!'

'Superdy duper,' said a nerd from one of the front rows.

'Nifty neat,' said another nerd.

There's more than one Nerd here? I thought.

'Now this is cool,' Mason said, turning to face me. 'What would happen if someone got stuck in the shuttle and it took off into space –you know, someone who wasn't an astronaut?'

'No one would be that stupid,' I said with a snicker.

'Yeah, no one could be that stupid,' Mason repeated, and we both laughed."

The crew members listening to Monty re-telling this story could not help themselves from cracking up. This kid was hilarious; he knew how to mimic everyone…he had talent!

CHAPTER SIX

"By the time we reached Montreal," Monty continued, "the bus had quieted considerably. The five-hour trip had done its magic, and most of the kids were asleep. I noticed Marlon the Melon drooling on the shoulder of Cody Musker, a huge, scary kid. *Oh no,* I thought, *Marlon's gonna get his melon head all squished up when Cody wakes up and finds drool on his jacket!*

"Miss Jenkins made her way to the back of the bus waking everyone up in turn, announcing that we were almost in Montreal. We all stared out the window. Everyone was exclaiming over the cobbled streets and the fact that all the signs were in French and English.

'Oui, Oui,' Mason said, poking me with his elbow.

'Pardon monsieur, qu'est que tu dit si'il vous plait?' I replied, smirking.

'Wow, he knows a lot of French,' Kerry whispered to her trusty sidekick Megan.

"Mason and I burst out laughing at this. . .they had no clue it was the only sentence I could remember from Madame Auberge's French class!.

"We arrived at the Space Agency Education Centre and filed out fairly quietly from the bus. After a head count had been taken, Miss Jenkins started to assign each one of us to a supervisor.

'Mason, Earl, Cody, Megan and Mark, you're with Mrs. Otto. Abdul, Kerry, Jennifer, Mary and Kendall, you're with Mr. Parton and Monty, Marlon, Peter, Dave and Kwame, you're with me!'

'That's not fair,' rang out fourteen voices all at once.

'I never get to be with Mary and Kerry,' whined Megan. 'I'm the only girl with . . . ,' she paused to count, '. . . three boys.'

'Four, Megan, four!' Mason yelled.

'And I always get to be in the teacher's group, I wonder why?' I said with a wink to Mason.

'Okay, everyone,' said Miss Jenkins. 'Let's have some peace and quiet here. You're in your groups because I want you to be in those groups. I'm expecting to have a wonderful time here and no one is going to spoil it for anyone else. Comprend?'

'Yeah, whatever,' Cody Musker said, under his breath.

'Yeah what?' Miss Jenkins snapped.

A low hum was heard that sounded like 'Cody's getting in trouble; Cody's getting in trouble, naa na na na naa.'

'Um, ah, yeah cool,' Cody said, looking quite afraid.

'It didn't sound like "cool" and I better not hear any grumbling or you're on the next bus back to Toronto. Do I make myself clear?'

"At the registration center, Miss Jenkins whipped out all her paperwork; she was a very organized person. We all checked in and got assigned a cabin number.

'Now listen very carefully; this is the schedule for today. We will unpack and then head towards the dining room for an early dinner. Afterwards, we will meet with our host Meredith, who will take us through the activities that we registered for. Okay?'

"On our way to the cabins, the groups fell apart and re-formed until everyone was with friends. Mason and I were talking about video games, Megan and Kerry were wondering why the sky was blue and the grass was green and not the other way around, and Cody was trying to bully Earl Parton without Mr. Parton seeing him. Marlon and Kwame were walking closely behind Mary and Jennifer... I think they like them"!

"I was in a cabin with Mason, and we were just unpacking our stuff—clothes anywhere, comics and electronic games neatly on the dresser—when there was a knock on the door. Earl peeked in.

'Hallo. Is this room 23?'

'Who wants to know?' Mason replied, a bit rudely.

'I do. I think I'm bunking with you.'

'You sure?' I said. 'You gotta be kidding. Um. . . .I'm not sure you'll like us.'

'I can learn. And who knows, maybe I can teach you guys some algebraic equations.'

"Mason and I looked at each other and mouthed NERD at the same time. Earl walked in and started unpacking his stuff: a microscope, mathematical set, a textbook of anatomy for high school and a bundle of clothes including a T-shirt that said *I used to be Einstein in another life!* He then took out all his underwear, neatly folded, and started putting them in a tidy pile in one of the drawers. All the while, he was humming the tune of Bill Nye the Science Guy's TV show.

'Hey Monty, have you seen my Super Mario game? I made sure to bring it and now it's missing,' said Mason, looking like he had lost his best friend.

'Naa, maybe it's under the bed or something. When you pulled everything out, it could have fallen down and been kicked under the bed by mistake,' I said.

'Hey, you think we could play some cool tricks on anyone? Maybe Megan and Kerry?'

'I don't think that would be decent,' Earl mumbled

'Who asked you, Einstein?' Mason said harshly.

'I was only being conversational,' Earl said meekly.

'Yeah, but you use weird words. If you talked like us, maybe we'd understand you better, huh?'

'Well, sure,' Earl said excitedly, 'I'll try.'

"Miss Jenkins' footsteps came down the hallway, and we heard her telling the other students to hurry to the dining room. I quickly grabbed two chocolate bars, put them into my pocket and left the room, with Earl following close behind. We fell in with the crowd heading for supper.

CHAPTER SEVEN

"After a huge meal of fries and chicken, it was all we could do to stop ourselves from keeling over right there in the dining room so we all promptly went to bed. I nearly had a heart attack when Miss Jenkins blew her whistle to wake everyone up the following morning.

'Why do we have to go anywhere? I just want to go to sleep,' Mason whined.

'Well, I for one can't wait to start participating in all these exciting, incredible experiments,' said Earl.

'Oh, here we go again,' Mason complained. 'I tell you, that guy can't talk normally and we have him in our room for three whole days?'

'Hey, he's not so bad,' I said cheerfully. 'Maybe we can get him to help us with our homework when we're back in school, huh?'

Mason looked at me with wonder, and then winked.

'That is… like… so good man. Why didn't I think of that?'

'Cos, you were too busy being mean to him and not realizing what he could do for us—as OUR FRIEND. He has so much POTENTIAL.'

'Ha ha, big word,' Mason retorted.

"We pounded each other's backs, then followed Miss Jenkins into a huge auditorium. There was a screen the size of a classroom wall with a picture of a space station. In front of us was Meredith, our host, and another lady in an astronaut costume.

'Wow, cool. I wanna go into space dressed like that.'

'Yeah, so you could beat everyone up by just knocking them over in your puffy clothes,' Mason interjected cheekily.

'Shhhh…respectful language, students,' Miss Jenkins said.

"It seemed like our teacher was in a trance. She was clearly fascinated by everything in the auditorium, and she had a faraway, dreamlike look in her hazel eyes.

"The agency's host cleared her throat and began.

'Hi, and welcome to the Canadian Space Agency. We are the leading centre in Canada for the study of Space Science and we work in collaboration with NASA and other Space agencies around the world, helping to promote the study of Space. Now, why would anyone want to study Space?'

"She looked around the room, obviously expecting an answer. Earl looked like he was having a fit, his hands waving madly showing how badly he wanted to be picked.

'Yes, what's your name young man?'

'Earl Parton, Madame.'

'Yes, Earl?'

'Well, we want to study space to see how it will help us live life on earth. It can help us expand our knowledge of other galaxies beyond what we can see from earth.'

'Wow! That was excellent,' said Meredith. 'He's exactly right. By studying how our bodies adapt to the space environment, we are able to determine how to create better drugs and how we can improve certain processes here on earth. Now, before we go any further, I would like to introduce you to someone famous, the first Canadian to visit the International Space Station …Julie Payette!'

"Everyone started to clap, and a young looking woman in an astronaut suit came forward with a huge smile.

'I wanna be like her one day,' Megan whispered to Kerry.

'Yeah, me too. Maybe the two of us could go off into space and discover new planets,' Kerry replied.

'Newsflash! You're both already there,' Mason whispered and I burst out laughed.

"Miss Jenkins overheard us, and shot over a look that could have turned a Wendy's Frosty into Campbell's soup. Then, Julie Payette started speaking.

'I'm so glad to be here and to be able to encourage you all to study hard, even if you don't end up studying science. I was born in Montreal and in high-school I scuba- dived, played racquetball and loved to sing. I studied really hard and won a couple of scholarships, eventually going to McGill University—one of the best universities in the country. After graduation, I worked for IBM Canada as a Systems Engineer and then was selected as an astronaut by the Canadian Space Agency in 1992. The training was hard work but a lot of fun too, like many worthwhile things in life. I went into Space on the Space Shuttle *Discovery* from May 27th to June 6th 1999 as part of the crew of STS-96; we went to help assemble the International Space Station. Space is beautiful. . .hopefully one day, at least one of you will be talking to other kids and telling them about your experiences as an astronaut.'

"The host, Meredith, spoke again. 'I would like to introduce you to another amazing woman, visiting our centre to train some of our scientists. Let's give it up for Dr. Mae Jemison!'

"We all clapped eagerly, and Mason gave a few war whoops as a beautiful African-American woman emerged from the side door, smiling and waving.

'It's so wonderful to be here in Canada with all of you and to look into the faces of some future astronauts,' she began. 'I was born in Alabama and got a scholarship to study at a university. Let me tell you, it wasn't easy at all. You know how it feels to work hard?'

A few hands went up.

'You know how it feels to do well?'

Another set of hands went up.

'Well, when you work hard and you do well, it REALLY feels good and that's what I've been trying to do all my life. You've got to have a plan, stick to it, get all the help you can along the way and keep your eyes on the goal!'

"Even though she was starting to sound like our basketball coach, she was pretty cool. Mason and I clapped along with everybody else when she was done. I couldn't wait to see the shuttle and explore the rest of the Space Agency.

"Then Meredith started a slide show that listed all the Space-related events of the past year—and there was a surprising number! I was startled by the fact that several asteroids pass dangerously close to the earth every day! How spooky is that? I have to warn Marlon. . .they could be aiming for his head! There were so many asteroids and they all seemed to be whizzing quite close to the earth in Meredith's photos

'Any questions?' Meredith spoke again.

"I couldn't help myself from blurting out: 'Have you ever been to space?'

"Meredith took the question seriously. 'No, I haven't. I'm working hard, though, and I hope to be chosen one day to train as an astronaut.'

'What does the space station look like?' asked Megan. Everyone turned to look at her like we couldn't believe she was capable of asking such a question.

'Well. . . what's your name?'

'Megan Genevieve Patricks.'

'Ok, Megan, good question. The International Space Station or ISS is a giant structure in space that has resulted from a partnership of 16 countries: Brazil, Canada, the US, Japan, Russia and 11 other countries, all in Europe. What this means is that 16 countries have come together to build one Space

Station, supplying all its different parts at different times. When it is finished, it will be about 400 kilometres above the earth, whizzing around at over 30,000 kilometres per hour with as much room in it as a 747 jumbo jet! The first module, or part, was the *Zarya* module that was sent into space by the Russian Proton rocket. Next, the shuttle *Endeavour* attached the *Unity* module to the *Zarya.* The third one was the *Discovery* shuttle, which sent in tools and cranes for the two modules already there. So you see, it's like a huge jigsaw puzzle with all the pieces fitting in, one at a time. Canada's major contribution, apart from sending in astronauts has been the Canadarm – an amazing robotic arm that assists the astronauts while they are at the Space Station. You can imagine that assembling the pieces on earth and then sending the large station to space would have been a daunting task. . . that's why they were sent up there bit by bit.'

"She stopped talking when another hand went up in the audience. Everyone turned to look at Kerry. Now this was getting more and more weird. What had those two been eating?

'Who are the crew members? Do they ever get to come home?'

'Well, the very first group had two Russians: flight engineers Yuri Gidzenko and Sergei Krikalev. Along with their American Commander, Bill Shephard, they were the first residents of the space station. The expeditions are timed not to go beyond six months. . . so, they must feel homesick at times, don't you think?

Marc Garneau, the first Canadian in space, was a crewmember on the STS-97, which was launched in 2000 on the shuttle *Endeavour*. They transported the Space Stations P6 Truss with the solar arrays that were used in a power distribution system. Although Mr. Garneau is now retired, he has logged over 678 hours in space.'

'Wow,' all the kids murmured.

'And that's not all. Other Canadians include Chris Hadfield, the first Canadian to walk in Space; Roberta Bondar, the first Canadian woman in Space and so many more.'

"After this explanation, Meredith brought out a huge basket of sealed plastic bags. Meredith, Dr. Jemison and Julie Payette started circulating and giving each of us a model rocket to assemble. After all the talk of shuttles, trusses and modules, it was great to put together a tiny replica of the *Soyuz* rocket. While we were all working, I saw Miss Jenkins make her way to Dr. Jemison with more questions.

"After about twenty minutes, Meredith clapped her hands and managed to get us all quiet. Most of the kids had assembled the rockets and were now fidgety.

'I'm going to send you off now to your cabins for some free time.' She paused at this point to let all the excitement die down. 'Tomorrow morning, you will all wake up at 7:00 am—'

'Noooooo,' we all groaned.

'—and make your way to the Space Lab. Here, you will perform various experiments and then take a tour of the facilities. As Miss Jenkins must have mentioned to you, we have an exciting launch here in Quebec, about 300 km north of Montreal. Some instrumentation is going to be transported to the launch site from this centre. We will all get to see the first Canadian launch of a space shuttle from the safety of this centre, and you will be amazed at the amount of energy generated—sound as well as light. So, everyone have a good night and see you tomorrow.'

As we left the auditorium, Miss Jenkins caught Mason and I trying to launch our rockets, complete with sound effects. When she was done lecturing us, the rows had emptied out enough for us to overhear a discussion at the front, where Megan and Kerry were talking animatedly with Ms. Payette. Miss Jenkins beamed with pride, until we heard Kerry's final sentence:

'Wouldn't it be cool to have an Astronaut Barbie?'

CHAPTER EIGHT

"The sun shone through cabin 23's window like it was trying to fight with the moon. Mason and I jumped out of bed and saw Earl tightly clutching his one-eyed Winnie the Pooh.

'Why do we have to wake up now? It's only 6:30 in the morning!' I moaned.

"But then something struck me. By now, my mom would have seen the note and she would be mad. Maybe I could impress her by calling home and apologizing. I got up, went to the washroom and cleaned my teeth; then I was off in search of the nearest payphone.

"I dialed, and held my breath when the phone at the other end started ringing.

'Hello?' said a familiar voice. .

'Hi Mom!' I said, trying to sound bright and alert, like it wasn't that early in the morning.

'Why on earth didn't you tell me what you were planning to do? Do you know how scared I was not seeing you home after school?' She sounded very much awake now. 'This is bad, Monty and I'm going to spend the time you're away trying to figure out what needs to be done with you. This irresponsibility is getting to be a bit much!'

'I'm sorry mom, and I won't let it happen again. We're going to be back on Wednesday so I'll see you then and make it up to you, okay?'

"I placed the phone back on the hook and went back to my cabin. Mason had already figured out that we couldn't use the television downstairs to play our games, but we'd come prepared with handhelds so start them we did. Poor Earl. . . the electronic noise was too much for him and he moaned in pain.

"Rrrrrrring! The bell went and then everyone was rushing out of his or her cabin towards the dining room. Mason and I each grabbed a backpack and filled it with snacks and video games. After a yummy breakfast of doughnuts and hot chocolate, we made our way to the auditorium. Miss Jenkins kept blowing her whistle like we were in the army. By the time we got there, the auditorium was full. There were two other grade six groups, from schools in Prince Edward Island and Quebec.

"Meredith was on stage again, wearing a cheery smile. 'Good morning everyone. I hope you had a restful night because you're going to be very, very busy today!' Earl and his friends gave a few muted cheers, while Cody and Mark dropped their heads and started muttering.

"Our class was split into groups and each group was assigned an Agency leader. We filed out of the auditorium and made our way to the laboratories. Mason and I were in separate groups AGAIN. Of course, we knew whose fault it was. . . Miss Jenkins's!

"Each of the groups had to perform an experiment related to Space. My group had to figure out how fast the typical nutrients in food are normally absorbed in the intestine. It was really cool—we got to eat different kinds of food, like fruit, bread, cheese and juice. Then we pricked our fingers with a machine that measured sugar levels in blood. We found out that juice sent the most sugar to our bloodstream in the shortest possible time. We were all supposed to take turns with the experiment, but of course Megan and Mary were squeamish.

'Why wouldn't you want to try? It's so cool,' said Cody, who was pretending to tattoo himself.

'I don't want to bleed to death, you know?' Megan replied in a shaky voice.

'But you have a lot of blood,' I tried explaining. 'You're not going to die from a few pin pricks.'

'Well, duh, who said?' Megan retorted. 'I've seen a man bleed to death before!'

I turned to roll my eyes in Mason's direction before remembering that he wasn't there.

"In another laboratory, Mason's group was trying to figure out how gravity worked. He told me all about it later. They used a canvas sewing needle to thread a string through a rubber ball. A knot was tied in the string on the outside of the ball to stop it from coming off. Next, the other end of the string was pulled through a straw and a roll of tape tied to that end of the string.

'Can I have a volunteer from this group, please?' said Giovanni, one of the Agency's Education Officers. He looked at the group and picked Mason.

'Uhhhhh, not fair,' whined Earl. Mason said he looked like he'd bitten into something sour.

'Okay, Mason. Hold the straw in the middle and swing the ball in a circle so that it orbits the straw. Keep your hand moving at a constant speed.'

"Everyone watched as Mason started, slowly at first but then building up speed. *This was fun*, he thought. *But, what did it mean?*

'Well, the path of the ball is called its orbital path,' said Giovanni, as if he could read Mason's mind. 'This orbital path is different for each planet. Now the string represents the force of gravity that holds the object in orbit around earth. Without gravity, what would happen?'

"Mary, who was cool and smart too and wanted to be a scientist one day, shyly put her hand up.

'Yes?' said Giovanni kindly.

'Earth would be out of control, and it would go flying off into space with no particular path,' she said proudly.

'Exactly! Now what would happen if we shortened the string or made it longer?'

'My turn, my turn,' said Earl, who was having one of his 'me, me, me' fits.

'Okay, why don't you try it and we'll discuss the difference.' After a few more demonstrations, Mason thought he understood orbiting planets. Basically, when planets are closer to the sun, they have shorter orbits.

"After about half an hour, the groups switched around so we would all get a chance to try every activity. Another experiment had to do with balance. We had to turn around in circles until we were dizzy, and then try to walk along a straight line painted on the ground. It was really tough! By one o'clock, I was beat. We had lunch, and then Miss Jenkins sent us to our rooms to rest.

CHAPTER NINE

"At three o'clock, Miss Jenkins startled us again with her annoyingly shrill whistle. She announced a tour of the facility, and had us lining up in front of the auditorium. Then we were led across the compound to an enormous metal building.

'This is where control of the aircraft takes place,' said Meredith, still acting as our guide. 'Everyone who works here is well trained to handle a crisis and many tests are done on the rocket and shuttle before take-off. If anything were ever to go wrong, it would be detected here first and then fixed. Now, let us move to the module that will house the astronauts.'

"We followed her, a bit awed, around the huge building. It took my group about twenty-five minutes to walk over to another large building, where we had to wait for all the slow pokes to catch up. She took us inside to a really cool area.

'This module houses an operations zone and a living zone. The living zone is where the crew members live, eat and wash. In this area, they have their own cabin, which contains a sleeping bag, chair and a porthole. The hygiene area contains a sink and shower.'

"A hand went up in the crowd. It was Mark— an annoying, sandy-haired boy.

'What happens to. . .you know. . .washroom stuff in space?'

'Eeewwwww,' said Jennifer. 'You are like…so…like…gross!'

'Yah' countered Kerry, Kendall and Meghan.

'Yeah, whatever,' Mark said, unconcerned.

'It certainly doesn't fly off into space!' replied Meredith, and I could tell she was trying to suppress a smile. 'It is stored and disposed off in a way that does not harm the astronauts or the environment.'

'Hey, maybe it goes into orbit, eh?' added Marlon.

'That would be so cool,' said Mark.

'Enough is enough! Let us move on,' Miss Jenkins said firmly.

"The cabins looked livable, although I was wondering where a television would fit. Next, the tour took us to the galley, which had a table, cooking elements and trash storage. In the control deck of the shuttle, I couldn't believe all the buttons and dials and monitors. *What were they all for?* Kwame, Kerry and Abdul got a chance to sit in the control chairs. Meredith pointed out that the straps were necessary for when the astronauts experienced a change in gravity.

'Wow, cool,' murmured Earl. 'I can't wait to be an astronaut.'

'I will allow you to walk around and look and touch stuff under the supervision of your parent volunteers, but no fooling around, okay?' Meredith said, sounding stern for the first time.

"We explored the cabins thoroughly, getting tired by six-thirty or so. There was a bit of free time before the campfire at eight o'clock.

"The campfire was a lot of fun. We all toasted marshmallows and crazy cheese, and even Miss Jenkins looked normal by candlelight. Everyone was talking about their favorite part of the day and when we held each others' hands and sang spooky campfire songs, it was sort of cool. . .not weird like it would have been if we were back in school. Miss Jenkins looked very happy, and said she was glad no one had done anything stupid – yet. Not even Cody, Mark, me or Mason. She seemed a bit surprised, actually. We got to bed pretty late that night.

"The next day was the shuttle's launch, and. . .you pretty much know the rest of the story. Are you gonna throw me out into space? Put me in jail? Will I have to serve time for trespassing in Space?"

Monty let out a huge sigh and stared at the three astronauts. They were silent for a few moments, until the senior officer spoke.

"You have learned so much already, we can't imagine finishing this trip without you. And, you're an amazing storyteller, you know? I don't think you left anything out. . .we feel like we know everyone in your class! I think you'll just have to stay here with us," said Ogden. "After all, there's no way we can send you back to Earth now. We're only in orbit for five days, so you won't miss too much school. We'll be orbiting the earth at very high speeds and recording some biological tests and then we'll return to earth. So, you're going to have to stay with us and you'll need a new name, too." He winked, changing his tone and sounding very serious, like he was announcing the start of a contest. "Let's see how it goes, Officer Bert Stein. Welcome on board the Space Shuttle *Experience*."

"Bert Stein?" Monty asked, confused.

"Well, of course," said Ogden.

"It's a play on Albert Einstein. . .do you like it?" Kirkpatrick added.

"Yah. . .I can live with it," smiled Monty.

CHAPTER TEN

Waking up was so easy on a space shuttle. At least, that's what Monty thought as he got out of his bunker and let his feet touch the floor. For a few minutes, he wasn't quite sure where he was and then he saw the porthole and his room's plain interior.

Could this really be happening? Officer Bert Stein on the Space Shuttle *Experience*? He wondered what his mom and friends were doing right now. Where was he anyway? He got up and went to the hygiene area to brush his teeth. The toothpaste was really funny tasting but it looked just like earth toothpaste. Monty made a mental note to ask them why it wasn't that different.

By the time he finished brushing his teeth, he heard one of the officers coming towards his room. *Actually*, he thought, *I shared a room with him.* He quickly ran to the bed and tried to make it look neat. It was harder than usual because the bed kept on flipping over, and Monty couldn't straighten the blankets while he was sitting on them. After a few futile minutes, he gave up. He didn't usually make his bed at home, anyway. This was one of the bad things he promised himself he would change. . .for his mom's sake!

Captain Edmonds walked in with a big package and handed it to Monty.

"Hey Monty, sleep well?" he asked in a friendly voice.

"Yeah, sort of," Monty replied. He didn't want to tell the captain that he was afraid of sleeping in a shuttle. "How come the toothpaste doesn't look that different on the shuttle?"

"Well, we're allowed to bring our own if it's approved," explained the Captain.

"And can I take a shower? Wash my hair?"

"Yes you can, with special shampoo. It's a kind that doesn't need to be rinsed out," said Captain Edmonds. "We're very lucky now to be able to take showers ALMOST like on earth, you know? The first showers developed by NASA for use in space had water floating all over the place. It had to be smeared on the body and then vacuumed off!"

"I would have loved that!" Monty laughed.

"Well, we've got to go up on deck and conduct a few tests, and we thought you'd like to come...hey, you can check your email too eh?."

"Wow, cool," Monty said excitedly. "like from hotmail? In outer space?"

"Well first, you've got to be properly dressed. I found an extra mission suit for you. Can you get undressed?"

Monty looked at the Captain like he was crazy. Get undressed with him watching? No way! Monty waited, stubbornly, until Captain Edmonds seemed to understand the situation, and he left the room.

Monty quickly got changed and called the Captain back in. The suit looked like it was from Star Trek. Monty couldn't help feeling a bit silly, especially since the suit was four sizes too big.

"Hey, cheer up; we didn't know we'd be taking a kid into space," the captain said.

"Yeah, sure," Monty replied glumly.

"This way," Captain Edmonds said as he led Monty from the cabin area onto the deck. This place really did look like Star Trek. It was majorly cool. He just couldn't imagine Mason's face if he told him all about this. He'd be so jealous!

"Hi Monty, wanna come over here?" Officer Kirkpatrick greeted him. Unfamiliar with movement in a shuttle, and weighed down by his suit, it took Monty at least five minutes to walk across the cabin's deck even though it wasn't that big.

The Officer pulled out a chair for him. They sat before a panel filled with buttons, similar to the ones Monty's class had examined earlier. Monty got excited at the thought that he'd get to find out what they were for!

"These buttons," said Officer Kirkpatrick, as if he knew what Monty was thinking, "are for running the shuttle and making sure we don't crash into things like asteroids."

"An asteroid? No way!" Monty said.

"Way! You know how many flying objects come towards us when we're in space? Debris is a serious hazard."

"What's debris?"

"Debris is basically rubbish, in this case, space rubbish. Some scientists worry that a really big asteroid could come close enough to the earth to be dangerous. It could even fall on a major city. What do you think?"

"I think that would be cool, except if it crashed on me. Maybe some aliens would come with it or something. Hey, you think we could see some aliens?"

The officers all laughed, and then they moved towards their monitors.

"Monty?"

"Yeah?" said Monty, turning towards Captain Edmonds.

"We've sent a message to earth, to the control centre in Montreal, to let them know that you're on board. We have arranged to have you communicate with your mom and then your school friends, so why don't you hang around until some connection has been made."

"You sure? Mom is going to be able to see me? Mason and Cody and Miss Jenkins will all be able to talk to me? How?"

"By satellite. We'll get hooked up in about ten minutes and you'll be able to speak to them at the control centre. Your mother is being taken down there too."

"How did you do that?" Monty asked.

"Well, after your teacher realized that you had accidentally left earth on the shuttle, she contacted your mother on her cell phone and asked her to come and meet them in Montreal. Everyone on your field trip had to get permission to stay for an extra day so they could speak with you and make sure you were okay. It sounds like Miss Jenkins is especially embarrassed that she let you out of her sight, so she really wants to make sure that you're alive and okay."

Oh boy, this was going to be a lot of fun. Even though he now knew that space was not really 'up there,' Monty did feel like he was on top of the world with all of his friends way below! As he was thinking of how jealous his friends would be, Monty saw Officer Ogden beckon him.

"Okay, we've made the connection, so get ready."

As Monty stared at the monitor, he saw the defined image of a man speaking through a microphone.

"Hi Alpha Titus Centauri, hold 3-2-7 under 3-2-2 over."

Yeah whatever, Monty thought. *This was like goobledegook.* He hoped he wouldn't have to speak to his mom and friends like that. Or maybe he'd make it up and pretend to his friends that he'd learned *astronautese.*

Then he heard his name. And he saw his mom, looking scared and very worried. It made Monty ashamed of himself. In all of the excitement, he'd forgotten how frightened his mom would be if he ever got lost. He really felt bad.

"Monty, honey, can you hear me?" she asked in a tremulous voice.

Silence. The officers all looked at him.

"Go on Monty," said the captain, "she's waiting to hear your voice and she can see you, so speak. It's like a webcam."

"Mom, I'm really sorry."

"That's okay, honey. You've been gone a while, you know? I know you're never going to be that silly again and I hope that you behave yourself in space and make me proud. You're the first astronaut in our family and the youngest ever in the world!"

"Yeah, I know," Monty said, starting to perk up. *He hadn't thought of that!* "What do you want me to bring back, mom?"

"I don't know. . . .You're not going anywhere near the moon, are you?"

"Ummm, I don't think so. Maybe I can bring you a souvenir from the shuttle?" he said, turning to look at the captain. Captain Edmonds nodded his assent. "I love you, mom, and I'll see you very soon, okay?"

Officer Ogden took over and continued receiving instructions from mission control while Monty turned his back to them. He didn't want them to see his eyes get misty. He missed his mom and his friends and what if he never got back to earth? With his kind of luck, it didn't seem out of the question.

"Monty, we're gonna have to wait to speak with your class so you can take a break and play some games. And oh, by the way, we found your backpack so you shouldn't be too bored," Captain Edmonds said, winking. That reminded Monty of Mason. He missed his friend a lot.

Monty ran to his cabin and realized that the captain had brought in his backpack earlier. He reached for it and pulled out his games, and for a bit, he forgot all about being homesick. Officer Ogden then took him to a part of the shuttle that he thought was the coolest – he got to float! Ogden passed him a screw driver and showed him how to use it to work on one of the instruments they were using to run tests. IT WAS SO COOL! Why didn't his school science lab look like this? He was sure he'd be getting A's all the time if he could float and do his experiments!

Back on earth, there was chaos. When Monty's mom finished talking to her son, she couldn't stop herself from crying. A tall, friendly lady led Mrs. Horton out of mission control into a quiet room and got her a hot cup of coffee.

"He's my baby, you know?" Monty's mom kept saying. "He's never done anything this stupid before." She took a sip of her coffee. "Actually, wait. That's not entirely true. There was the time when. . . ."

"That's okay, Mrs. Horton. The three officers are good men and they'll take care of him. We will arrange to have you stay at one of the downtown hotels, and you can speak with him every day until they come back. It's Thursday morning now and they'll be back on Tuesday, so it won't be long."

This seemed to calm her down enough to stop her tears.

CHAPTER ELEVEN

According to the shuttle's computers, it seemed the astronauts had been in orbit for three days. Monty was playing a game on the YTV website when Ogden told him that they were ready to connect to earth again. It was his chance to speak to his school friends! His entire class had been invited back to Mission Control, and they were going to see him in space.

"*Experience* to Mission Control 8-7-4 over."

"Mission Control to *Experience* 4-7-8 over."

The screen started taking form and there was his whole class!

"Hi Monty," they all screamed in excitement.

"Hi everyone," Monty replied, grinning. He couldn't quite believe his eyes. Everyone was smiling at him, even Miss Jenkins. She didn't look that mad. At least, he didn't think so.

"Hey Monty, you're so cool. How come I never think of wacky things like you do?" Mark hollered. The class nodded in agreement and laughed, although Miss Jenkins looked at Mark a little disapprovingly.

"Hello Monty," said his teacher. "I hope you'll have plenty to tell us when you return. We've missed you and we're very proud that one of us will be the first child astronaut."

"Yah punk!" said his best friend Mason who couldn't keep still. "Hey, come down quick 'cos I've got to show you this game."

"Do they have Barbies in space, Monty?" asked Megan.

"No, Megan. But I've been floating and doing experiments – its so cool in zero gravity!."

As Monty listened and answered the class's questions about what it was like to be in space, he felt lonely. He missed them already and he couldn't wait to be back.

"I'll be back soon, guys," he said to the monitor.

"You better hurry, Monty," said Earl in his squeaky voice. "We're done with the Space Unit and Grade Six will be over in five days."

"What?" Monty said, startled.

Before Earl could respond, the screen blinked and went dark. Monty turned to look at Ogden.

"What did Earl mean by that?" he asked, trying to keep the worry out of his voice. "The part about Grade Six being over? It's only January!"

None of the astronauts would look at him. He felt tears stinging his eyes and he though he wanted to disappear. Just at that moment, one of the computer monitors started beeping. *Wait a minute*, he thought, *are we going to crash?*

It was an email – sent especially to him from Earl to his email address <u>montyhorton@hotmail.com</u>.

Earl said algebra was over (he actually wished he was there for it!) and Miss Jenkins was now the strictest teacher ever – because she thought everyone would be naughty like Monty – no hall passes ever again – even if you were dying to pee!

"Come sit here, sonny boy," Officer Ogden said.

The Officer moved Monty over to a comfy couch in another section of the deck and sat down beside him. On the counter beside the couch was a photograph.

"You know this guy, right?"

"Yeah. That's Einstein. Albert Einstein."

Officer Ogden continued, "Well, Einstein was really smart and won the Nobel Prize in Physics for a discovery about light and how it travels. He also came up with a theory to describe how light travels in space. He told anyone who would listen that the sun has such a strong gravitational pull that light skimming its surface gets distorted."

"Wait a minute," Monty interrupted, "what does 'gravitational' mean?"

"Gravity is a property or something that a body has that pulls it towards something else. Our bodies are pulled by gravity to the earth and that's why back on earth, we don't float in the air. If we were on a mission to the International Space station to fix something, we'd be out of the shuttle and in Space where gravity is virtually non-existent. In that case, we'd be floating because there'd be nothing to pull us to the earth."

"Gotcha," Monty said. "Gravity makes sense, but what's 'distorted'?"

"Well, that's when something is forced to change its direction. For example, if I told you to walk over to that chair by the third monitor, you'd walk straight towards it, wouldn't you?"

Monty nodded.

"Well, what if I put three huge beanbags in that pathway so you had to go around it? Your path would be distorted, because you're not going in a straight line, but you'd still get to where you're going, right?"

"Right!"

"Okay. Einstein's theory was tested in 1919 during a solar eclipse and—guess what? Another scientist called Eddington produced data that indicated that Einstein *might* be right. The light that passed by the sun seemed to get distorted by the sun's gravity. Einstein's theory of special relativity led to other theories about space bending and time contraction. Because we are traveling at a speed that is very fast, we seem to be losing time. So, at this time, it seems like your friends are ahead of you in time and have almost finished the grade six year, but because you are in a place where there's little gravity, time seems to have slowed down very much. Basically, what we physicists like to call your inertial frame is changing while the inertial frame of your classmates isn't changing because they're still on earth. When you get back home, try googling 'twin paradox' okay?"

"Does that mean that when I go back, they'll be in Grade Seven and I'll still be in Grade Six?"

"Naaa. As we get back into the earth's atmosphere and gravity becomes effective, our speed will slow down and it will seem to get us back into real time."

"This Einstein guy was so cool, eh?" Monty said.

"Definitely. He also came up with an equation that we can demonstrate to you – right here on the space craft. It's called the $E=mc^2$ equation, and in its simplest terms, means that if anything that has mass was to travel at the speed of light squared, in a vacuum, it should immediately turn to energy and vice versa."

"What? You mean if I traveled at the speed of light squared, I would turn into energy? How?"

"Well, theoretically, the molecules in your body would be moving so fast that they would turn into energy—pure energy. But remember, it'd have to be in a vacuum!"

"Can we try that?" Monty asked eagerly.

Monty was taken to another room on the shuttle and within the twinkling of an eye, he felt himself go woozy and then…he disappeared! And then he reappeared. And then he disappeared! Like 5 times!!!!!!!

This was awesome. How did Einstein think of these incredible things? How could he possibly get one of these E=mc2 machines on earth...cos it could come in VERY handy when he had to disappear from one of the scenes of his many crimes!

As he continued to teleport himself and any other thing he could lay his hands on, Monty didn't feel bad anymore that his class could be ahead of him, because he realized that everything was relative. It just *seemed* that time had gone more slowly because he was traveling at a fast, constant speed in a very low gravity environment.

Monty said good night to the other officers and made his way to the cabins. He was going to write in his journal so he would remember everything that had happened.

Before he could start writing, however, he fell asleep.

CHAPTER TWELVE

Monty felt like he was falling down a long tunnel, hearing the Captain's voice saying "Einstein" over and over as he was falling. He woke up with a start and found himself in his bed at 225 Spyglass Crescent, on earth, panting like a dog.

That was the most awesome dream of his life!!

The clock on his wall read 3 a.m. Ordinarily, Monty would have just turned over and gone to sleep. Right now, though, he was too excited—he felt alive and full of energy. All of a sudden, he knew what he was going to put on his science fair poster, and it was going to blow Miss Jenkins's mind. He couldn't wait!

Slowly, he crept out of his room, switched on the computer in the family room and googled "Canadian Space Agency." He put it under his favorites and then googled "NASA for kids." Into favorites it went. Then using his favourite drawing software *Inspiration©*, he gradually made a smaller version of what he wanted his poster to look like. He was so pumped he didn't see his mom staring at him from the top of the stairs.

"Oh, hi Mom," he said cheerily.

"What are you doing up so early, Monty?"

"The name's Officer Stein, mom. And, I'm designing a poster for the Science Fair next week."

"Well well," said Dana Horton. *What had she given him for dinner last night? She should definitely stock up on it!*

Monty felt like he had a glow around him as he got on the bus for school. As the day wore on though, he found it hard to focus after his early morning start and the strange, exciting dream of the night before.

"Hey, wake up sleepy head," Mason whispered, just as a spitball from Cody's huge pen came flying across the room.

Monty looked up and tried to look wide-awake as Miss Jenkins walked slowly and deliberately toward his desk. His body was in the classroom, but he felt his mind was somewhere else…and he felt sooooo sleepy!

"Perhaps Monty Horton will do us the favor of sharing his science fair project plans?" Miss Jenkins couldn't keep a slight sarcastic tone out of her words.

"Ummh, right," Monty stammered, glad for a chance to invite his mind back into his head! "I have my field trip form signed too, Miss Jenkins". He eagerly handed it to her – there was no way he was going to miss the field trip he had just dreamed about!

"I see. Do go on, we're all listening," Miss Jenkins prompted as she looked suspiciously at his signed form.

"I've decided to study Special Relativity because although it's not well understood, it is an example of how science works. Someone thinks of an idea, proposes a theory and tests it—and then it may get accepted by a lot of people but not everyone. And, even though it doesn't get accepted by everyone, we see evidence of the theory all around us. We all know Einstein was famous because he won the Nobel Prize in Physics after experimenting on the way light behaves in different environments."

Monty took a deep breath.

"He also thought that if a body with mass moved away from the earth's gravitational field at a fast, constant speed, it would seem to lose time and be much further behind in time than a similar body on earth. He called this idea his Theory of Special Relativity, in which he said that light from distant planets is distorted when it passes by the sun because of the sun's gravity."

Monty was starting to sweat, and he was a bit worried about the strange look on his teacher's face. He continued,

"Well, it's a bit like when you are in a train or subway car which has come to a stop and another train passes by. Anyone felt like *their* train was moving?" Lots of hands shot up.

Monty got up, brought his poster to the front of the class and placed it on the easel Miss Jenkins had in front of the board. All eyes were on him and they were certainly all ears! Monty had never sounded so smart before!

"Space is so cool that we need to spend time figuring out how it works. It just might help us live better on earth!"

To say Miss Jenkins was flabbergasted would be an understatement. She was so shocked by Monty's speech that she couldn't help rewarding him with a hug. In fact, she almost choked him to death!

Monty looked around the class, and everyone looked as astonished as Miss Jenkins. Even Earl was impressed, quickly passing him a note that said, "I think we can be friends."

When Monty put the note in his pocket, his hand touched something. He pulled out a small, square package: it was strawberry-flavoured, freeze-dried ice-cream.

The kind astronauts eat in space.

Well, what do you know Monty?

About the author

Mary Asabea Ashun received her Ph.D. from SUNY Buffalo and has taught for several years in Ontario's public and private school systems. She is currently an Assistant Professor in the Department of Education at Redeemer University College in Ancaster, Ontario.

Original Cover art: RACUD
www.globalillustration.com

Coming Soon!

NEW!

How can Isaac   Newton's universal theory of gravity be demystified?

The Adventures of Monty Horton as Zach Newton!

Monty tries out for the track team but can't quite make the 13 second dash that Dan Marfo clocks. Maybe high jump will make him famous. Read to find out what happens when gravity takes control of Monty's dreams to get on Kingsway Middle School's Hall of Fame!

Made in the USA